PUFFIN BOOKS

Roll Up! Roll Up!
It's Rita

Roll Up! Roll Up!
It's Rita

Written and illustrated by
Hilda Offen

PUFFIN BOOKS

For Jodie Patterson

PUFFIN BOOKS

Published by the Penguin Group
Penguin Books Ltd, 27 Wrights Lane, London W8 5TZ, England
Penguin Putnam Inc., 375 Hudson Street, New York, New York 10014, USA
Penguin Books Australia Ltd, Ringwood, Victoria, Australia
Penguin Books Canada Ltd, 10 Alcorn Avenue, Toronto, Ontario, Canada M4V 3B2
Penguin Books (NZ) Ltd, Private Bag 102902, NSMC, Auckland, New Zealand

Penguin Books Ltd, Registered Offices: Harmondsworth, Middlesex, England

First published in 1998
3 5 7 9 10 8 6 4

Copyright © Hilda Offen, 1998
All rights reserved

The moral right of the author/illustrator has been asserted

Typeset in Bembo Schoolbook

Printed in Hong Kong by Midas Printing Limited

British Library Cataloguing in Publication Data
A CIP catalogue record for this book is available from the British Library

ISBN 0-140-38698-X

It was the day of the school fair.

"I hope we win the fancy dress competition," said Jim.

"I'm going to have a balloon ride first!" said Julie.

"Can I be the back legs of the dragon?" asked Rita.

"We'll think about it," said Eddie.

Rita went to feed the rabbit. While she was gone, Julie's friend Tania came round with her brother Eric.

They all ran away together.

Rita found a note stuck to the fridge.

"Sorry, Tich," it said. "Your legs are too short."

Rita was furious. Then she had an
idea.

"I've already got something to
wear!" she said and she raced upstairs
and changed into her Rescuer's outfit.

She set off for the fair.

"Oh, look, Grandma!" cried a little boy. "There's a girl dressed as the Rescuer! I wish I could be her! I wish I wasn't a rabbit."

TO THE
FAIR

Rita joined the people crowding into the school field. The first thing she saw was a toddler having a tantrum.

"I promised him a coconut," said his father, "but I can't manage to hit one. I think they're glued in, anyhow."

"Let's see what I can do," said Rita.

BOING! BOING! BOING!

The coconuts flew left, right and centre.

"How's that?" said Rita.

"Time for the sheepdog trials!" announced someone over the loudspeakers. "Shep McDuff will now round up all the sheep and herd them into the pen."

Mr McDuff blew his whistle.

But something was
wrong – the sheep were
behaving very strangely.
They gnashed their teeth and
started to chase Shep round
and round the ring.
Shep was terrified.

"Stop it!" cried Mr McDuff,
but it was no use. The
sheep looked fiercer than
ever and chased Shep
into the pen.

"This is a job for the Rescuer!" said
Rita.

First she rescued Shep and handed
him to Mr McDuff. Then she darted
about the ring rounding up the sheep
while the people cheered and clapped.

Soon all the sheep were safely in the
pen. Rita spoke firmly to them and
they hung their heads and bleated.

"You can start again," she
said to Mr McDuff.
"They've promised to
do it properly this time."

Across the field, the weightlifters were getting restless.

"Where's the football team?" they asked. "They're late for the tug-of-war."

"They're all down with German measles!" cried the judge. "We shall have to cancel the contest!"

Rita stepped forward.

"Can I take the place of the football team?" she asked.

"Oh, would you?" said the judge.

Rita pulled the weightlifters across the line with her teeth.

"What strength!" cried the crowd. "What amazing jaws!"

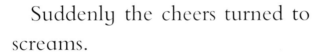

Suddenly the cheers turned to
screams.

"The hot-air balloon is falling!"
someone yelled. "Look out!"

It was true! The balloon and its
basket were hurtling downwards.

"Help!" screeched Eddie.

Rita streaked across the field like an arrow. She caught the basket just before it hit the ice-cream queue.

"A magnificent catch!" said Mr Lorenzo. "Have an ice lolly."

Eddie tottered out of the
basket followed by the others.

"Please, *please* can we have your
autograph, Rescuer?" begged Julie
and Tania.

"Not now," said Rita.

She'd heard a muffled voice calling,
"Help! Help!"

The maypole dancing had come to
a standstill. Miss Smiley, the
reception-class teacher, was all tangled
up in the ribbons.

"Leave this to me," said Rita. "Can
you play 'Over the hills and far
away'?" she asked the band.

Rita's toes twinkled and the ribbons
turned to a blur of colour.

"What grace!" cried the onlookers.
"What skill!"

Rita danced faster and faster. Soon
Miss Smiley was unwrapped.

"Oh, thank you, Rescuer!"
she gasped. "I wish you were
in my class!"

"Roll up! Roll up!" It was the announcer again. "See the amazing Ollie Osborne on his motorbike! See him do a handstand on the saddle! See him jump through a blazing hoop!"

There was a roll of drums.

"See him leap over six lorries!" cried the announcer.

VROOM! VROOM! Ollie zoomed up the ramp. He flew through the air.

"Oh no!" gasped the crowd.

Ollie had fallen off his bike!

"Here I come!" called Rita.

She caught Ollie in one hand and the motorbike in the other and set them down safely on the grass.

"Bring me another six lorries!" said Rita. "Now, Ollie, watch carefully!"

"Wow!" cried the people as she soared through the air like an eagle.

"What a performance!"

After that, Rita had a go at the
sideshows. She played skittles, she
climbed the greasy pole, she rang the
bell and she threw the wellington boot
further than it had ever been thrown
before.

She won a real live pig, fifty pink rabbits, twenty teddy bears and twelve fluffy elephants.

She gave the toys to the children in the crowd. And she gave the pig to Mr McDuff who was very pleased and said he would keep it on his farm.

"Time for the fancy dress competition," said the announcer and everyone surged towards the stage.

"Third Prize," said the mayor, "goes to Tracy Thompson for her cat outfit.

"Second Prize goes to Wayne Watson for his octopus suit! And First Prize – goes to – RITA THE RESCUER!"

Everyone cheered while Rita stepped up to receive the gold cup.

"Thank you!" she said.
"Got to dash!"

At the back of the stage she spotted Eddie, Julie and Jim standing with Tania and Eric.

"I thought your costumes were great!" she whispered. "Here you are – have this!"

And she handed them the cup. Then she whizzed off into the blue sky.

Rita was in the back garden when the others got home.

"Sorry we left you behind, Rita," said Julie. "You missed the Rescuer again!"

"We thought you'd like this," said Jim.

It was the gold cup!

"Look inside," said Eddie.

Rita lifted the lid. The cup was filled with strawberries!

"Mm! Lovely!" she said. "Thank you, everyone!"

Also available in First Young Puffin

BEAR'S BAD MOOD
John Prater

Bear is cross. His father wakes him up much too early, his favourite breakfast cereal has run out and his sisters hold a pillow-fight in his room. Even when his friends arrive, Bear just doesn't feel like playing. Instead, he runs away – and a wonderful chase begins!

GOODNIGHT, MONSTER
Carolyn Dinan

One night Dan can't get to sleep. First of all he sees a strange shadow on the wall. Then he sees huge teeth glinting and hairy feet under the bed. It couldn't really be a monster – could it?

RITA THE RESCUER
Hilda Offen

Rita Potter, the youngest of the Potter children, is a very special person. When a mystery parcel arrives at her house, Rita finds a Rescuer's outfit inside and races off to perform some very daring rescues.